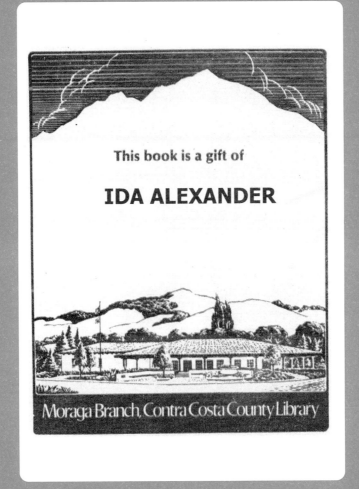

*Keep rolling—
and reading!
Barbara Odanaka*

SKATEBOARD MOM

Barbara Odanaka

ILLUSTRATED BY

JoAnn Adinolfi

G. P. PUTNAM'S SONS

It all started on the day I turned eight.
I was opening presents—all of them great.

But when I unwrapped the gift from Aunt Di,
That's when I noticed the gleam in Mom's eye.

"A skateboard?" she said. She flashed me a grin.
"A SKATEBOARD!" she said. "May I go for a spin?"
My friends started giggling. My ears turned red.
Mom grabbed my helmet and plopped it
     on her head.

"See you later," she said, skipping out the door.
"See you later," she said, not a single word more.
"Hold on!" yelled Granny. "Turn around! Come back!"
But Mom zipped down the sidewalk, clickety-clack.

Clickety-clack.
Clickety-CLACK.

Rolling along like a train down a track.

CLICKETY-clack. Clickety-CLACK.

Picking up speed and not looking back.

"Whatcha gonna do?" asked my best buddy, Tom.
"Whatcha gonna do 'bout your skateboardin' mom?"

Yikes! I thought, as my mother whizzed by,
Popping an ollie on her very first try.
She pulled off a spin so high in the air,
It knocked all the curl right out of her hair.

Clickety-CLACK.

Clickety-clack.

"Mom,
    can I have my
    skateboard back?"

Clickety-clack. CLICKETY-CLACK.

"Please,
    may I have my skateboard back?"
She didn't even hear me.
    Her eyes were kind of glazed.
She kept saying "Awesome!"

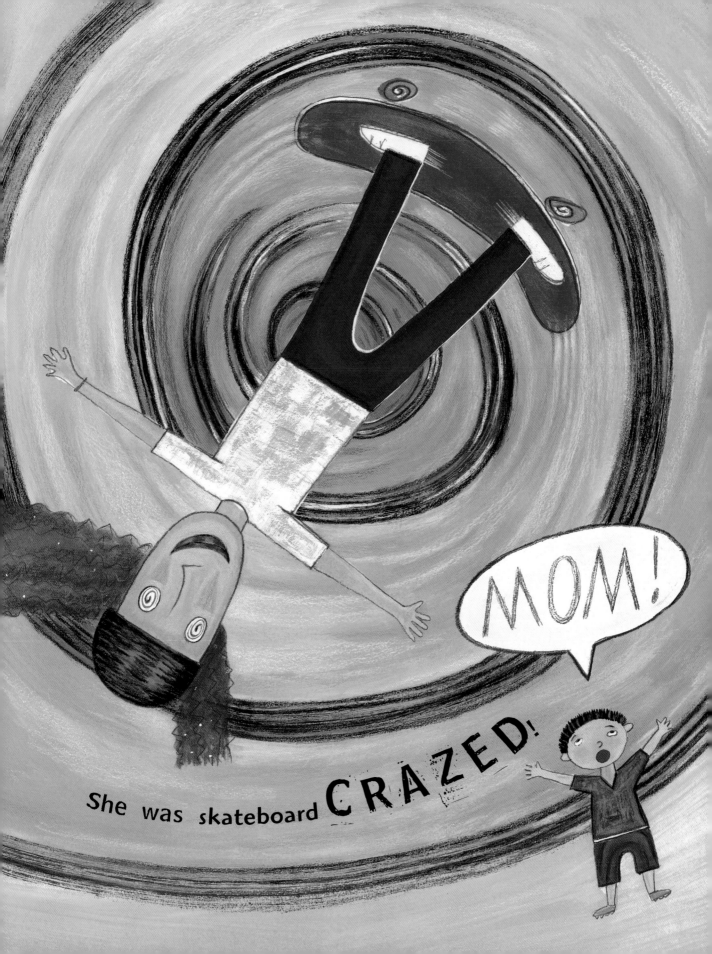

She was skateboard CRAZED!

"Mom," I said. "Would you trade for my bike?
My baseball cards, or my horned toad, Spike?
You don't want those? Well, how about these:
A scooter? Stilts? A flying trapeze?"

"Be patient, son," Dad said with a smile.
"Your mother hasn't skated for a long, long while.
 She used to be a champion, your dear ol' mom.
 She even rode her skateboard to our Senior Prom.

"And when it was time to walk
    down the aisle?
Your mama chose to g l i d e,
    skateboard style."
Right then and there, I knew what to do:
I grabbed my piggy bank and off I flew.

When I got back—
WOW—what a scene!
"It's HER!" a man cried.
"The skateboard QUEEN!"

I pushed through the crowd. I caught Mom's eye.
She skidded to a stop and said with a sigh:
"I'm sorry, son. Oh, where do I begin?
I lost my head. It won't happen again—"
"Mom," I said. "I thought you were GREAT.
Would you, could you, teach me to skate?"

She squeezed me tight. I handed her the gift.
The wood was strong; the wheels were swift.
"Oooh, sweetheart . . ." was all she could say.

We hopped on our boards to roll away—

"WAIT A MINUTE! STOP! HOLD IT RIGHT THERE!"

It was Granny, shouting, fist in the air.
She grabbed my board. I heaved a great sigh:
Granny—dear Granny—had a gleam in her eye.

For my parents. —B. O.
For Gemma and Hans. —J. A.

Manufactured in China by South China Printing Co. Ltd.
Designed by Marikka Tamura. Text set in Highlander ITC Medium.
The artwork for this book was created with pencil, gouache, watercolor, colored pencil, and pastel on watercolor paper.
Library of Congress Cataloging-in-Publication Data
Odanaka, Barbara. Skateboard mom / Barbara Odanaka ; illustrated by JoAnn Adinolfi.
p. cm. Summary: An eight-year-old boy gets a skateboard for his birthday, but when his mom tries it out,
she has so much fun that she won't give it back.
[1. Skateboarding—Fiction. 2. Mothers and sons—Fiction. 3. Stories in rhyme.]
I. Adinolfi, JoAnn, ill. II. Title. PZ8.3.O275 Sk 2004 [E]—dc21 2001008525
ISBN 0-399-23867-0
3 5 7 9 10 8 6 4 2